WILLOW VALLEY

Toffee Apple Night

Tracey Corderoy

Illustrated by Hannah Whitty

First published in the UK in 2013 by Scholastic Children's Books
An imprint of Scholastic Ltd
Euston House, 24 Eversholt Street
London, NW1 1DB, UK
Registered office: Westfield Road, Southam, Warwickshire, CV47 0RA
SCHOLASTIC and associated logos are trademarks and/
or registered trademarks of Scholastic Inc.

ISBN 978 1 407 137612

A CIP catalogue record for this book is available from the British Library.

Printed and bound by CPI Group (UK) Ltd, Croydon, CR0 4YY
Papers used by Scholastic Children's Books
are made from wood grown in sustainable forests.

1 3 5 7 9 10 8 6 4 2

www.scholastic.co.uk/zone
www.traceycorderoy.com

For Alana, with love. . . x

T.C

WILLOW VALLEY

STUMPY'S STYLE

BUTTON-OAK MILL

POPPY FIELD

PODRICK HARE'S HOUSE

TEN OAKS FIELD

ALLOTMENTS

BUTTERCUP MEADOW

MOSSY HOLLOW

HORATIO'S HOUSE

WILLOUGHBY WHITE-WHISKERS' HOUSE

ACORNS SCHOOL

LIBRARY

BLUEBELL WOOD

VILLAGE SQUARE

BAKERS

STARLA'S HOUSE

TOY SHOP

HOOT HILL BARN

MUMFORD MOLE'S HOUSE

THE DARK WOOD

MARTHA RABBIT'S HOUSE

OLD CROOKED STONE BRIDGE

RILEY'S HOUSE

Chapter 1

Autumn had come to Willow Valley in a whirl of sweet woodsmoke and berries. Red and orange and deep yellow leaves danced down from the trees, and shiny brown conkers dotted the soft, wet grass.

Riley, a little toffee-coloured mouse, was on his way to school, helping himself to the big purple berries filling the blackberry bushes. With him were his two best friends – Starla, a smiley, fluffy-faced badger, and a roly-poly hedgehog called Horatio Spark.

"Mmmm," smiled Riley as he nibbled another berry. His fluffy little face was stained with juice and his small pink nose was all sticky. The first berries of autumn were such a treat!

"Hey," grinned Horatio. "Save some for me. After ginger cake, you know, berries are my favourite things!"

"You say that about *everything*," Starla giggled.

It was true. Horatio liked lots of things. Tightrope-walking was one of them and snacking was definitely another! He also liked adventures, and though he *tried* to be good, Horatio nearly always ended up in trouble. . .

The friends filled their mouths with so many blackberries that their cheeks puffed out like balloons. Then off they raced down the hill, the whole of the valley stretching out before them.

Riley saw ribbons of thin white smoke curling up into the sky. It was coming from little caves all over the hills. But these were no *ordinary* caves. They had neat, round windows, thick wooden doors and wibbly-wobbly chimney pots. They were the cave-*houses* where the animals of Willow Valley lived.

Riley liked his cave-house very much. The kitchen often smelled of baking bread and there were big, soft rugs on the floor. The thick stone window sills were filled with woodland flowers crammed into jam jars and jugs. And just beside the fire was a big, cosy

rocking chair where Riley and his little
sister, Mimi-Rose, read stories.

Down in the valley, Riley spied the
village square. It looked tiny from so high
up! And there was their school beside
Library Cave and his grandpa's toy shop.

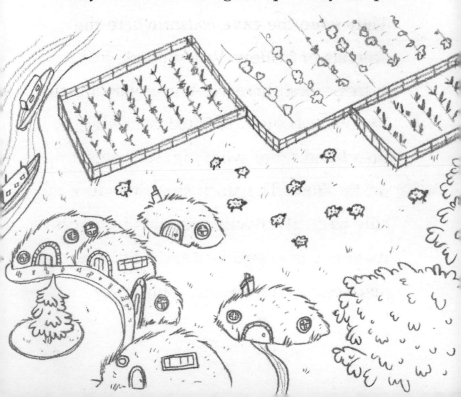

In the distance the neat, square fields spread out like a patchwork quilt. And the hills were dotted with sheep as fluffy as rain clouds!

As the friends reached the bottom of the hill they heard the soft tinkle of the river. A bank of willow trees swayed in the breeze, dropping feathery leaves. Then three big narrowboats came into view, bobbing about on the cool, clear water.

The *Whirligig* was at the front. Its dark blue paint twinkled in the early-morning sunshine and around its windows were paintings of beetles and pink roses.

Behind it was the *Dragonfly*. This was a dark green boat with a bright red door. It was decorated all over with small, lacy-winged dragonflies.

Then Riley saw the *Kingfisher*. This was his favourite boat. It was sky blue with a big bright kingfisher painted on its bow. Riley hoped one day, when he was an explorer, he would have a boat just like this!

These were the boats that the animals used to go on their market trips when they'd sail downriver to sell home-made goods. For their next trip Riley's mum was going to make blackberry jam – if

Riley and his friends left any berries on the bushes!

Suddenly Starla spotted her grandpa, Willoughby White-Whiskers. He was on board the *Kingfisher* with lots of busy little helpers. Some were hammering, others were sweeping, and Willoughby held a tin of paint.

"Grandpa!" called Starla. "What are you doing?"

"Oh hello, Starla," smiled the wise old badger. "Just smartening up the boat for the Riverside Festival!"

In two days' time the Riverside Festival would be taking place by the river. This party happened every year and was held to celebrate the start of autumn. The narrowboats always started it off by parading down the river.

Riley and his friends called the festival *Toffee Apple Night* because it happened at night and they'd get to eat yummy toffee apples!

No one loved Toffee Apple Night more than Riley. He loved being out after dark with his friends, all huddled around the big bonfire. And he loved all the fun things he'd get to do – whizzing down the giant helter-skelter, toasting marshmallows, and last year he'd been the apple-bobbing champion!

Riley also loved watching the firefly parade when fireflies would dance through the dark night sky, their bright little bottoms glowing like shiny jewels.

Willoughby checked his pocket watch. He still had quite a lot to do if the boats were to be ready in time. And because he was the captain of the fleet, it was up to him to make sure it all got done.

"Goodness!" said Willoughby. "Is that the time?" He glanced down his long list of jobs.

"You three had better get a move on too, or you'll be late for school."

Then suddenly he saw their whiskers dripping in sticky purple berry juice. "Been scoffing blackberries again?" he smiled.

"Just a few!" Starla giggled back.

The friends waved goodbye, then raced off to school. The bell was ringing as they arrived and they flew through the gate like little rockets.

"*Phew!*" puffed Horatio, his cheeks bright red. "Just in time!"

Their teacher, Mumford Mole, opened the classroom door and everyone pattered inside. They hung up their scarves and popped their lunch boxes on the shelf.

When they were all sitting down,
Mr Mole called the register. Then
he asked everyone to take out their
planning books.

"We're doing something special
today," he said.

"Oooo! I know! I know!" cried
Horatio, bobbing up and down in his
chair. "We're making our figurehead
thingies, aren't we?"

"For Toffee Apple Night!" smiled Riley.

Mr Mole nodded. "Yes, that's right.
Well remembered!"

Everyone took out their planning
books. Then Mr Mole reminded them

that Toffee Apple Night was to celebrate all the good things the valley gave them at harvest-time. . .

"Wheat for our bread," he said. "Berries for our jam (*and* for our sneaky morning snacks!)." He pointed at Riley's sticky purple nose and chuckled.

"Who can think of *more* harvest-time goodies?" Mr Mole asked.

"Juicy carrots!" Bramble Bunny smiled.

"Nuts fall from the trees at harvest-time!" cried Abigail Bright. Being a squirrel, she liked nuts very much.

"*I* fall from the trees at harvest-time, too," grinned Horatio, nodding his head. "I fell out of two whole apple trees last night!"

Everyone laughed. They were so excited about Toffee Apple Night – especially the figurehead competition which the children of Willow Valley took part in every year. The winning figurehead would lead the narrowboat parade. It would sit on the bow of the front boat as all three sailed down the river.

"OK, quieten down now," Mr Mole said. He showed them some pictures of figureheads to remind them what they were. "The Vikings had figureheads on their boats, see?" he smiled. "They were models of things, mostly made out of wood. And they used them to decorate the front of their longboats."

He pointed to the figurehead in the picture he was holding. It looked like a big wooden sea-monster.

"But that looks really hard to make!" said Riley.

"Don't worry, Riley," Mr Mole replied. "Your figureheads don't need to be that tricky. Think back to the ones you made last year. Now, can anyone remember what we *use* to make our figureheads?"

"Leaves and twigs!" smiled Posy Vole. "We scoop them up with our paws!"

"Conkers," little Phoebe Badger nodded.

"*Glitter*," gasped Riley. He loved using glitter *so* much.

Mr Mole smiled. "That's right!" he said. "We use things from the woods to *build* our figureheads. Then we smarten them up with bits and bobs we have here in the classroom. Things like glitter, buttons, ribbons, beads and—"

17

"—toilet paper!" Horatio cried. "We twist it into flowers and stuff."

"*No*," snorted Starla, giggling like mad. "That's *tissue* paper!"

Riley thought of last year's Toffee Apple Night. A big, bright peacock had won the figureheard competition. Bramble Bunny's group had woven it out of willow canes and its tail feathers were lots of painted oak leaves. It had looked so special leading the boats downriver, while fireflies in all the colours of the rainbow had twinkled overhead. It had been the *best* night ever!

Suddenly Bramble put up his paw. "Which boat will be the leader this year?" he asked.

"The *Kingfisher*," Mr Mole replied, and Riley's eyes grew wide. How brilliant would it be if *his* group's figurehead led the parade on his very favourite boat!

"Right then, children," said Mr Mole, "quietly get into groups of four and start planning out your figureheads. Oh, and very good luck to you all!"

"Hooray!" cheered everyone. There was a buzz of excitement as the children picked their groups. Everyone *loved* making figureheads for the competition!

Riley, Horatio and Starla had little Digby Mole in their group. No one else seemed to want Digby, who was ever so quiet and shy, so Riley said he could be with them.

"Thanks," said Digby timidly, his spectacles slipping down his nose. Then each group pushed their desks together and sat down.

Riley opened his book and looked around. Suddenly his whiskers drooped. Rothwell was sitting in the group *right* behind them.

Rothwell was a mean, slate-grey
mouse who always picked on Riley. Last
summer he'd *even* entered Riley into the
Big Bike Race when he'd known full
well that Riley couldn't ride a bike!

In Rothwell's group was a water vole
called Columbus (Rothwell's only friend)

and two girls – Abigail Bright and Posy Vole. Neither of the girls looked very happy at having to be with Rothwell, but he and Columbus were the only ones left.

Rothwell glowered at Riley. "Oi, Riley!" he hissed. "Get ready to lose this competition!"

"*Hey*," frowned Horatio. "Leave Riley alone."

"Make me!" smirked Rothwell. "*We're* going to win. You lot don't stand a chance!"

"Huh," said Starla crossly. "We'll see about that!"

Chapter 2

"So what shall our figurehead be?" asked Riley. It had to be something really good.

"Hmmm," said Starla, sharpening her pencil, "something no one's done before."

"I've got it!" beamed Horatio. "Let's do a *ginger cake*. But instead of using twigs and stuff, let's bake a *real* cake instead. Then after the parade we can all *eat* it!"

"But that's not allowed," Starla giggled.

"Nope," grinned Riley, shaking his head. "Mr Mole said we must use things from nature – fir cones and conkers and stuff. Ginger cake's made from eggs, flour and milk."

Suddenly, Digby put up *his* paw. He'd had an idea too.

"Um," he muttered quietly. But Horatio was *far* too busy imagining a great, yummy ginger cake figurehead.

"—But flour's from nature!" Horatio butted in. "Eggs are too. So is milk! A ginger cake model would be the BEST!"

"Um," muttered Digby, a tiny bit louder.

"But what if it *rains*, Horatio?" said
Riley. "The cake would go all soggy."

"It won't rain!" boomed Horatio.
"And anyway, it could have an *umbrella*
on top."

"Um," Digby muttered again, but
suddenly Starla leapt up.

"Hey, guys – I know!" she cried. "Why not do a *firefly* figurehead? The parade always has *real* fireflies, so our model would be perfect! We could make it from twigs and moss and fir cones, and use glitter to make it all sparkly."

"Cool," Riley nodded.

"But, but. . ." muttered Digby.

"*Oooooh*," groaned Horatio grumpily. Frowning, he curled into a prickly ball and wouldn't talk to anyone until Riley tickled his feet and he popped open again, giggling.

Starla opened her book and started to

sketch out the firefly idea. "Sticks for the body, and moss," she said.

"And don't forget the glitter on its . . ." Riley stopped and sniggered, ". . . *bottom!*"

As they carried on planning Rothwell kept leaning over, pretending to need rulers and sharpeners.

He was *spying*. Riley was sure of it!

"Quick! Hide our work!" Riley whispered to his group. "I think Rothwell's trying to copy."

"The cheat!" scowled Horatio, his prickles pinging up so he looked like an angry pincushion. Then he and Riley built a big wall of books around them.

When everyone's sketches were finally done they got ready to walk to Bluebell Wood. Now they needed to gather up the things to make their figureheads.

"Everyone get a basket," Mr Mole said, "and line up by the door."

"Yippee!" squeaked Riley. When he grew up he wanted to be an explorer and a trip to the woods was like going on a real expedition!

They lined up and Mr Mole led them outside, through the playground and past the big pumpkin patch.

Near the potting shed was a little wooden gate. The children filed through it, chattering excitedly, then headed up the hill to Bluebell Wood.

On the way they passed Starla's cave-house. Her mum was in the garden raking up the leaves as they tumbled down off the big plum tree.

"Mum!" called Starla, waving wildly. "We're off to find things for our figureheads!"

Starla's mum smiled. "Here, have some lovely leaves!"

She scooped a bundle into her great big paws and hurried to the wall. Starla and the boys ran over and put the leaves into their baskets.

"Thanks!" they said. Those leaves would come in very handy!

With that, Mr Mole called over and they rushed to catch up with their classmates. Rothwell's eyes narrowed when he saw their leaves. Then Riley saw *him* gather up a few leaves too.

The children carried on up to the wood in a nice, neat line. But the very moment they stepped inside. . .

Ping!

Ping!

Ping! Their fluffy ears shot up

and their sweet little eyes grew wild.
Now the race was on to gather the best
things for their figureheads!

"*Twigs!*" Bramble Bunny bellowed to
his group.

"*Moss!*" shrieked Phoebe Badger.

"*Leaves!*" yelled a hedgehog.

"*Pebbles!*" boomed a vole.

"*Pillow. . .*" yawned a sleepy little
dormouse.

Badgers dug holes to find good
stones, while moles snuffled round for
conkers. Then a group of squirrels shot
up an oak tree to search out
the shiniest acorns.

Bit by bit, the baskets began to fill up,
but Riley's group still hadn't finished.
And then, as Starla collected up moss,
she spied Rothwell peeping out from
behind a big rock.

When Rothwell thought she wasn't looking, he tiptoed out and grabbed some moss too. Then he quickly stuffed it into his basket.

Starla gasped, then hurried to her group.

"Riley! Horatio! Digby!" she panted. "I think Rothwell's copying us – collecting exactly the same things as we are."

"Hmmm," said Riley. There was only one way to find out. . .

Making sure Rothwell's group could see him, Riley gathered up five shiny conkers and popped them into his basket. A moment later he noticed Rothwell do just the same!

Next, Horatio picked up a bunch of twigs and two big, round pebbles. A few seconds later, pretending to fall over, Columbus did *exactly* as Horatio.

Finally, when Digby fished an acorn from the leaves, Rothwell found one too. He slipped it into his basket when he thought they weren't looking.

"Cheats!" scowled Horatio under his breath.

"That's so not fair," tutted Starla.

"Don't worry, though," said Riley as Digby's whiskers drooped. "We can *still* build a much better figurehead. And we will!"

Back in the classroom that afternoon the children started making their figureheads. Whether Rothwell was copying or not, Riley's group wanted to do their very best!

First they made their firefly's body out of twigs and bendy willow canes. They took great care with their loops and ties until it was just the right shape. Then they stuck on moss to fill in all the gaps.

"Now for its face," Riley said. He carefully glued on two pebble eyes. Then Horatio did a big conker smile.

"And look," said Starla. "Digby's made some wings!"

She helped him tie them on the firefly's back. Then Digby showed how they opened and closed.

"Wow, they look like they're really flapping!" said Horatio.

Now their firefly needed a sparkly
bottom, so they plastered its tail in
thick dollops of glue, then shook on
a rainstorm of glitter. Blue, green and
bright silver sprinkles covered their
books, their paws, and their *teacher*! Mr
Mole's glittery nose gave a wiggle. . .

"Aaa-chooo!"

"Hey, we mustn't forget *our* firefly's
nose," Riley told the others. So Digby
(who had turned out to be great at
making things) glued the acorn nose on
neatly.

"Hooray!" cheered everyone. Finally
they had finished!

They tidied up, and as they did, Riley looked around at the other models. Some of them were really good too.

Bramble Bunny's group had made a rocket which was blasting out tissue-paper flames. There was also a good mermaid Phoebe's group had done. She had long green hair made from moss and wore little fish hair clips made from pink and lilac sequins.

Riley couldn't work out what the other models were. They had twiggy bits shooting out in all directions – rather like Horatio's prickles!

"I think our figurehead might win,"

whispered Starla.

Secretly Riley did too. But then. . .

"*Oh look,*" Horatio groaned. "*Over there!*"

Riley spun around and his jaw
dropped. Rothwell's group's figurehead
looked *exactly* like theirs, even down
to its little acorn nose! So Rothwell *had*
been copying them all along.

"Do you like our firefly?" Rothwell smirked, and Riley felt his cheeks turn red.

"Well, ours is better," said Horatio bravely. "For one thing its nose is on straight!"

"And ours has a *way* more sparkly bottom," Starla nodded.

With that, *ding-a-ling* went the bell. It was time to go home. They wouldn't find out who had won the competition until Toffee Apple Night, the day after tomorrow.

As they left, Riley turned and glanced at the fireflies again. Really his friends were right. Their model was a *lot* more sparkly and the nose on Rothwell's was wonky. He just hoped whoever was judging the competition liked nice, straight noses!

Chapter 3

The next morning at school, Riley spied Rothwell creeping out of the classroom.

"*Look*," he whispered to Starla and Horatio. That wasn't allowed. Mr Mole always told them that no one should go in until *he* did.

Just then, their teacher strolled out of the staffroom and opened the classroom door. "In you all go, then," Mr Mole said with a smile.

Everyone pattered into the classroom. But Riley had barely stepped inside when his eyes grew wide and he stopped.

"*Oh no!*" he cried, pointing a paw. "Look!"

One of the figureheads was in bits on the floor. Riley recognized it at once. But now it was all crumpled and bent.

"*Our firefly!*" he gasped. He could hardly believe it. Their lovely, sparkly firefly was ruined.

Suddenly Rothwell came slinking up. "What a shame!" he tutted. But Riley could see he was hiding a smirk.

"It must have toppled off the desk last
night," said Rothwell.

Riley stared at the firefly. Then slowly
he looked up and pointed at Rothwell.

"H-he did it, Mr Mole," Riley stuttered.

"Did you *see* Rothwell break your
model?" asked his teacher.

"Well . . . no," said Riley quietly. Rothwell was glowering now.

"But we saw him coming out of the classroom!" Horatio blurted out.

Mr Mole nodded thoughtfully. "Hmmm, I see. . ." he said. "But that doesn't mean he broke the firefly."

"Yeah," grumbled Rothwell. "Riley's always blaming me for everything!"

Rothwell sighed and pretended to look upset. Mr Mole turned to look at him.

"So, if you didn't break the model, Rothwell, what *were* you doing in the classroom?"

"That!" Rothwell answered at once, and he pointed to Mr Mole's table. On it sat a shiny red apple.

"I brought it for you, Mr Mole," said Rothwell. "The biggest apple off my tree!"

"Oh!" said his teacher. "Well, um . . . thank you, Rothwell!"

Suddenly Riley felt his whiskers ripple crossly. Rothwell was lying. He *had* broken their model. And he'd done it to make sure *his* won! He'd only left an apple in case he needed an excuse.

Horatio knew it too. He edged up to Rothwell. "You did wreck our model. I know it!" he whispered.

"So what if I did?" Rothwell whispered back. "Mr Mole believes *me*, not you. Ha!"

Meanwhile, Starla had gathered up their firefly and placed the bits on the table by the window.

"Can't we mend it, Mr Mole?" Riley asked.

"Yeah," said Horatio. *"Please?"*

"I'm sorry – maybe later," Mr Mole replied. "Right now you all need to write a story about how you made your figureheads."

"Nooooo." Horatio curled into a ball. "Not *writing*!"

Mr Mole told everyone to get out their writing books and fill their inkwells with ink. Then they all got on with writing their stories, even a gloomy Horatio.

The morning dragged on for Riley. He kept glancing at their firefly all in bits. And Rothwell kept catching Riley's eye and smirking.

After lunch Riley asked Mr Mole again
if they could try to fix their model.

"We could do it really quickly,"
Starla said.

"Yeah, like a flash!" cried Horatio.
"I'm super-fast at glittering *and* gluing!

And I won't glue myself to my chair again. *Or* paint my paws in lots of glue and pick it all off when it's dry. Because I *am* really sorry that I did that before, Mr Mole."

Their teacher listened. Then he shook his head.

"I'm very sorry, Horatio," he said, "but it's maths time now."

"*Nooooo*." Horatio curled into a ball. "Not *maths*!!"

After maths time it was story time. Then *ding-a-ling* went the bell and it was suddenly time to go home.

"But what are we going to *do*?" sighed

Riley, as he and his friends put on their scarves. It was too late. Toffee Apple Night was *tomorrow*. . .

Riley plodded out of school. He hadn't felt this glum since his birthday when he'd fallen in the river. Horatio, Starla and Digby looked crumpled too.

"Rothwell can't get away with this," moaned Horatio. "There must be *something* we can do."

Digby nodded.

"There isn't," sighed Riley. But Starla had suddenly stopped.

"What?" said Horatio.

"Well," replied Starla, "there *might* be something we can do after all!"

She thought for a moment. And as she did, a smile spread from whisker to whisker.

"We could make *another* figurehead – tonight!" she cried. "Something even better than the firefly!"

"Like what?" squeaked Riley. His ears pinged up and his nose gave a twitch of excitement.

"Um! Um!" said Digby, his paw in the air. He'd had this idea since yesterday morning and now he was *bursting* to say it.

"I know!" Digby yelled at the top of his voice. "I know what we can make!"

Suddenly everyone jumped in surprise.

"*You do?*"

"Oh yes!" cried Digby. "I do! I do!"

Digby's tiny eyes twinkled as he whispered his plan to the others. . .

"*Wow*," gasped Horatio.

"Cool!" Riley nodded.

"Great idea, Digby!" smiled Starla, and they arranged to meet at Riley's house right after tea to get started.

"Bring any bits you have at home," said Riley, as Rothwell suddenly barged past.

"*Bits?*" said Rothwell. He stopped in his tracks and spun around to glare at Riley.

"Bits for what? What are you up to?"

"Nothing!" grinned Riley. Then he and his friends hurried off up the hill. They didn't have a single moment to waste!

Chapter 4

Starla, Horatio and Digby met Riley in his den after tea. Then Digby showed them a drawing of his figurehead idea.

"That dragon's *so* cool," gasped Horatio.

"He's even breathing fire!" cried Riley.

"What's he made from, Digby?" Starla asked.

Digby snatched up a stick off the floor. "I'll show you!"

Little Digby Mole had never looked

prouder. He tapped the drawing with his stick.

"His body," said Digby, "is a hollowed-out tree trunk. And his head is the same – just a bit higher up!"

Next, Digby tapped the fiery flames shooting out of the dragon's mouth.

"His flames are made out of twigs," he said. "Curly willow branches would be good because they're wibbly-wobbly. We'll have to put lots of glitter on them too. Red and orange and gold."

"Oh yes!" cried Starla.

"Are its wings made from twigs, too?" asked Riley.

"No, they're bits of *fir tree*," Digby nodded.

"Good idea!" said Horatio. "But he does need a name. I say we call him, um . . . *Ernest*."

The others weren't sure about that name, but Horatio said it was perfect.

"Because dragons say '*Er*' when they growl," he said. "And they keep their eggs in a *nest*. So what do you get when you put *Er* and *nest* together? *Ernest!*"

Everyone laughed but thought that was clever. So Ernest became the dragon's name.

"And what are those things on his tail?" asked Riley.

"Those are his scales," Digby replied. "We could use conkers for those."

"Hey, I've been collecting conkers," said Horatio. "I've brought them all with me, look." And he poured a pile of them out of his rucksack. "There!"

The dragon's eyes would be acorns covered in glitter. "Maybe green for the eyes?" said Digby. "But I didn't have any glitter at home so I just brought the acorns."

"Don't worry!" said Riley. "I've got some glitter. It's in the making-things box I share with my sister."

Starla had brought a big bunch of twigs and some more crunchy leaves from her garden. She showed them her basket which was filled right to the top!

Now they had to go and find a hollowed-out tree trunk, some curly willow for the flames, and some nice green bits of fir tree for the wings.

They raced out into the garden and Riley got a wheelbarrow to put everything in. Then Starla and Digby saw a hollowed-out tree trunk lying by the fence. They called Riley over and loaded it into the wheelbarrow.

Meanwhile, Horatio had collected some curly willow branches from under the tree by the pond. He popped them into the wheelbarrow, along with a rosehip from the bush by the shed which he thought could be Ernest's nose.

"There!" said Digby, adding two fir tree branches. He checked all the bits and smiled. "I think we've got everything we need!"

It was getting quite dark and chilly now. "Let's make Ernest in my cave-house," said Riley. He wheeled their things into the kitchen, where the lanterns had been lit and a roaring fire crackled in the grate.

Riley's mum was stirring a pan of toffee which smelled of big bright bonfires! On the table nearby were apples on sticks, waiting to be dipped into it.

"Oh, toffee apples!" Horatio beamed. "Are those for tomorrow night?"

"Yes, Horatio." Riley's mum nodded.

"So, not for . . . *now*?" Horatio asked, his eyes big and hopeful.

"Tomorrow night!" chuckled Riley's mum. "And you'll like them all the more if you have to wait."

"But I like them *already*," Horatio gasped. "I *LOVE* them!"

Suddenly a little snowy-white mouse skipped in from upstairs. She was dressed like a ballerina, but wore stripey socks and fairy wings too.

"Riley! Riley!" squeaked Mimi-Rose. "Why have you got a tree trunk?"

Riley's little sister gave a wobbly twirl, toppled over, then rolled about giggling.

"Ooops," grinned Riley. "We're going to make something special!"

Riley's mum looked over from the stove. "Oh," she said, "what?"

"A dragon figurehead!" Riley nodded. "It's for the competition."

Riley made Digby show her his drawing.

"Oh, Digby," she smiled, "clever you!" And Digby's cheeks turned as red as the apples on the table!

"So now we've got to *build* him," said Riley. He hurried over to the big oak dresser and took out the making-things box.

"Right then," Riley nodded, "let's get started."

Everyone's whiskers rippled with excitement as they started to make their model. First they did the body, then the wings. Then they glued on Ernest's flames.

Next, Mimi-Rose gave the little dragon two small stripey-socked feet. "Now he can dance like me!" she squeaked brightly.

When all of Horatio's shiny brown conkers had been glued on to Ernest's tail, it was time to get on with the very best job – the glittering!

They plastered the wibbly flames with glue. Then everyone grabbed a pot of glitter.

"Ready?" beamed Riley. "On your marks, get set – *GO!*"

Suddenly the air was filled with twinkles as everyone shook on their glitter. Mimi-Rose had silver, Starla had gold, Horatio had orange, Digby had yellow, and Riley had *two* pots of red. Soon Ernest's flames sparkled like the fire in the grate!

Then Digby dusted the dragon's eyes with green glitter, before Riley stuck on the red rosehip nose.

"Yippee!" cheered everyone. Ernest was finally done!

With that, Riley's mum came over carrying a big bunch of toffee apples. "A special treat!" she said with a smile. "As you've worked so hard."

"*Whoa*," gasped Horatio. "After ginger cake, you know, toffee apples are my favourite things!"

"Ah yes, Horatio," chuckled Riley's mum. "I thought so!"

The friends tucked into their toffee apples and for once it went all quiet as five sticky little mouths nibbled away.

Just as they were finishing, there was knock at the door, and Riley rushed over to open it.

It was Starla's grandpa, who had come to take her home, along with Horatio and Digby.

"Grandpa!" called Starla. "Come and see what we've made!"

Willoughby came in and they showed him Ernest.

"He's for the competition!" said Riley. "Because our other figurehead got broken."

"And a jolly fine fellow he is too!" smiled Willoughby as he gazed at Ernest's twinkly flames and his little stripey socks.

"Well, of course I'm not the judge," he said, "but I really do hope you win."

"Me too," gasped Riley.

"And me!" said Digby proudly.

Chapter 5

The next morning Riley's friends called for him to help carry Ernest to school. The day of the Riverside Festival had finally arrived!

Riley's mum and Mimi-Rose waved from the door as everyone headed off.

"Bye," called Riley excitedly. "See you later!"

School was finishing an hour early today. Then everyone was meeting at Hoot Hill Barn where the children would leave their figureheads to be judged. After that the whole village would head to the river to get things ready for the party later that night.

Riley loved getting the party ready. "I'm going to find good sticks," he said, "and help build a great big bonfire!"

"Oh me too," Digby nodded.

"I'm helping my grandpa with the tent," said Starla. Every year they put up a big tent where the toffee apples were served. There were lots of little craft stalls in there too.

"I'm going to set out the toffee apples," said Horatio, puffing out his chest importantly. "I might have to *test* some too, just to check they're OK!"

As soon as the friends arrived at school they went to the staffroom to find Mr Mole and show him their lovely new figurehead.

"My, my!" smiled their teacher, examining the dragon. "He's blowing out a fine lot of flames! And did you make him by yourselves?"

"All by ourselves!" Riley nodded. "We didn't have a single bit of help."

"Well, apart from Riley's sister," said Starla. "But she's really little."

"Ah, yes – I see," smiled Mr Mole. "That's fine, then."

The friends put Ernest on Digby's desk for the day and the little mole guarded him fiercely – *especially* when Rothwell came anywhere near.

Like yesterday, time went very slowly.

Riley couldn't wait to be setting up the party. He was counting down the minutes until the end of school.

Finally it got to, "Ten minutes to go. . ."

Then, "Five. . ."

And then, *"Twoooooo!"*

At last, *ding-a-ling* went the bell. It was time to go! "Yippee!" cheered Riley, jumping up from his desk.

The children gathered up their figureheads to take to Hoot Hill Barn to be judged. Then Mr Mole led them out and up the hill.

When they got to the barn a big group of animals were already gathered inside.

The children placed their figureheads on long wooden tables ready for Podrick Hare to judge later.

They wouldn't find out who had won the competition until the start of the narrowboat parade, when the winning model would be displayed on the front of the *Kingfisher*.

"Good luck, Ernest," Riley whispered, but it looked like Rothwell had smartened up his firefly. Its nose was on straighter. Its wings were more sparkly. And now they opened and closed.

"*Oooh*," tutted Digby. "He's made it so good."

"Hey, Ernest's good too," Riley said.

"*Yeah*," cried Horatio, patting Digby's
back.

"Ernest is great!" Starla nodded.

Everyone headed downhill to the river
to get things ready for the party. When
they arrived, they got to work right away.

The squirrels used their big, bushy tails to brush up dry leaves for the bonfire, while the rabbits bounced as high as they could, hanging bunting in the trees.

A group of badgers then set up the helter-skelter under the watchful eye of Podrick Hare. And hedgehogs, voles, moles and mice speared marshmallows on to willow canes to be toasted in the bonfire later.

As Riley and Digby were gathering sticks, Starla spotted her grandpa. The tent was about to be put up and Willoughby was gathering helpers.

He already had a big group of badgers and voles.

"Anyone else?" Willoughby called.

"Us!" cried Starla. She grabbed Horatio's paw. "Come on!"

They ran over and everyone got to work, passing poles and hammering in pegs. It took quite a while but at last the tent was up.

Lanterns were then hung in all the trees and the bonfire was built nice and high. It wouldn't be lit until it was dark. Toffee Apple Night would only begin when the very first star was spotted in the sky.

"Oooh!" squeaked Riley. "I hope that's really soon!"

It was now time to stop for a little break. The animals all gathered on logs by the riverbank with mugs of warm milk and ginger cake. Riley sat between Starla and Horatio and watched as the boats were sailed upriver, ready for the start of the parade.

"You know," said Riley with a big, cakey smile, "I think this is my very best kind of day!"

After tea, Horatio headed into the tent and helped set out the toffee apples,

taking sneaky little nibbles when no one
was looking (just to test them!).

Riley and Starla met him later in front
of the helter-skelter. They all liked the

helter-skelter so much. It was red and white, and as tall as a lighthouse, with stairs going up to the clouds!

You climbed the stairs with a rough brown mat, right to the very top. Then you'd sit on the mat and whizz back down a whirly wooden slide until you reached the bottom all red-faced and dizzy!

Riley looked up to the top and smiled. "I can't wait to go down it later."

"Me too," said Starla.

"And me!" cried Horatio. "Though I don't like the mats – they're so prickly."

"Not nearly as prickly as *you* are!" Starla giggled.

On top of the helter-skelter was a flag.
The friends watched it flutter in the
breeze. It was starting to get colder and
darker now. Not that anyone minded.
The darker it got, the better it would be to
see the firefly parade. Then suddenly. . .

"*First star!*" Riley yelled, pointing a
paw to the sky.

"First star!" gasped a squirrel.

"First star!" beamed a mole. "Riley Black-Paw's spotted the first star of the night!"

"Hooray!" cheered animals everywhere. "First star!"

Now that the first star of night had been seen, it was time for the festival to begin! Soon fireflies would be dancing over the twinkling water like a shower of sparkling stars. Then the bonfire would be lit and the smell of woodsmoke would fill the dark night sky. It would cling to gloves and scarves and whiskers, and make everyone feel warm inside.

Riley watched as the lanterns in the trees were lit. Then a big silver moon peeped out from a cloud and little winking stars popped out everywhere.

"Oooo!" he squealed as he wrapped his scarf around him. It was time!

Chapter 6

Riley and his friends clapped their paws.

"Yippee!" cried Horatio. "It's starting!"

As he bounced up and down there was a patter of feet. Then something small came flying through the grass and crashed right into him – *bump!*

"Ouch!" squeaked Digby. "Prickles! Oooo! Horatio . . . is that you?"

Digby had lost his spectacles and had been worrying he'd never find his friends.

"Yes, Digby," Horatio giggled. "It's us!"

Digby's whiskers quivered as he squinted towards the river. "The competition," he gulped. It was time to find out who had won.

With that, a voice came over the loudspeaker. It was Podrick Hare. . .

"A very warm welcome to the Riverside Festival, or Toffee Apple Night if you like! I'm happy to say that I've chosen the winning figurehead and it's on the Kingfisher right now!"

"Oooh!" came an excited gasp from the crowd.

"Oh yes!" said Podrick. *"And the boats are upriver, all ready and waiting to parade.*

So take your places at the riverbank and let's begin!"

Everyone scurried to the riverbank to get the best spot. Riley and his friends got right to the front and stood with his mum and little sister.

"Ooooh!" Mimi-Rose squeaked, jigging about in fairy wings, earmuffs and wellies. She clapped her paws excitedly. "Who will win?"

Riley and his friends were wondering that too. It could be the rocket Bramble Bunny's group had made. Or Phoebe's group's long-haired mermaid. Or it might be Rothwell's very sparkly firefly. . .

And then, in the distance, Riley heard the chug of the boats' engines. "They're coming," he whispered.

"I know!" squealed Starla. "Fingers crossed!"

A moment later, they spotted three boats in the distance gliding down the river. Above them a swarm of twinkling fireflies danced through the dark night sky, their sparkly little bottoms glowing like fairy lights!

There were red ones, purple ones, green, blue and pink ones. There were lilac and golden ones too! Some were zooming up with a *whoosh*, while others spun round like wheels. The tips of the fireflies' tails shot out stars which fizzed, sparked and popped! And the air all around was filled with a screechy. . .

WHEEEEEE!

Starla liked the lilac fireflies best, which danced like ballerinas. Their twirls were as graceful as tumbling autumn leaves and she watched as their pretty, petal-soft wings shimmered in the silvery moonlight.

Horatio preferred the bright red fireflies that wiggled and jiggled and zipped through the sky like they had ants in their pants!

"'*Cor*," he gasped. "I wish *I* could fly like that!"

Riley's favourites were the blue ones. These soared about like flying saucers, changing colour as they went. One minute they were blue, then purple, then green, then the colour of golden honey.

"Now silver!" cried Riley, as they changed yet again. *"Oh wow!"*

The crowd "oohed" and "ahhhed" as they watched the bright show. But Riley's eyes suddenly shot to the *Kingfisher* as Willoughby sailed her into view. And there, on her bow, what should he see, but. . .

"Ernest!" gasped Riley. He rubbed his eyes, for he could hardly believe it.

"Look!" he shouted. "It's Ernest! We've won! *We've won!"*

Horatio leapt up into the air like one
of the zippy red fireflies. "Hooray!" he
cheered, as Starla swung Digby round
and round in the air.

As she did, Digby's lost spectacles
tumbled out from the folds of his scarf.

Riley caught them, popped them on to Digby's nose, and *he* saw Ernest too. Then the shy little mole let out a giant. . .

"WHOOPEE!"

Riley had never been more excited. Suddenly he felt a warm, fuzzy feeling drifting up from the tip of his tail to the tops of his fluffy brown ears.

"And the winning figurehead. . ." said Podrick Hare, *". . . is Ernest, the stripey-socked dragon – made by Riley, Starla, Horatio and Digby!"*

"And Mimi-Rose!" squeaked Mimi-Rose. "I did the socks!"

Everyone cheered. All except Rothwell, who was stood with Columbus, scowling.

"This is *your* fault, Columbus," Rothwell hissed. "You should have put more glitter on our firefly!"

"Oooh," sighed Columbus, hanging his head. "Sorry, Roth."

Rothwell glowered over at Riley. But Riley didn't care. As the narrowboats sailed past, the bonfire was lit. Now it was time for some fun!

"Let's do some apple-bobbing!" Riley cried.

They hurried off to the apple-bobbing stall. Hector Rabbit was running it tonight.

APPLE BOBB

He showed them to a barrel filled with cold water. On the top of the water were lots of rosy apples bobbing about brightly.

"You have to stand on this," said Hector, pointing to a small round stool. "Then you pop your head into the barrel (not under the water, mind!) and see how many apples you can nibble. And remember – no paws are allowed."

"We know – I remember from last year!" Riley smiled.

Starla went first but try as she might, she couldn't catch any of the apples. Every time she got near they bobbed away.

"I think I'll bring my fishing net next year!" she grinned.

Riley went next. He was good at this. He slowly edged his face into the icy water and nosed the apples to the side of the barrel. Then he nibbled and nibbled and nibbled with all his might!

Digby just wanted to watch so finally it was Horatio's turn. He took a deep breath and plunged his head into the barrel.

SPLASH!

A great big fountain of water shot up into the air.

More water spilled out over the sides
as Horatio nosed the apples around,
making gigantic ripples.

"Silly apples!" he spluttered. "Come
back here!" Then he tried to *spear* them
on his prickles instead.

"Disqualified!" chuckled Hector
Rabbit.

"Well, I don't care!" grinned Horatio.
"It's marshmallows time! Look – over
there!"

He pointed to the bonfire and they
pattered across. Then Riley's mum
helped them toast marshmallows
in the crackling flames.

"Mmmm," smiled Riley, as he nibbled his down. It was yummy!

Everyone had more, and more, and more. Then it was time for a mug of parsnip soup with a chunk of warm crusty bread. Of course, pudding would be the toffee apples later on.

The friends all played a game of conkers under the lantern-lit trees.

"I play them with my brother, Ralph," said Digby. "And I win nearly all the time. *Especially* when Ralph loses his spectacles. Hee Hee!"

As they played, Abigail and Posy came up. They said that Ernest was a really good figurehead and they were glad he had won.

"And we didn't know Rothwell had been copying you," said Abigail. "Not until it was too late."

"And we certainly didn't know he'd wrecked your firefly model," added Posy.

She said they'd hated being in Rothwell's group. And that Abigail and Rothwell had argued all the time.

"He even said I'm *bossy*!" boomed Abigail.

"That's OK," Riley smiled. It was all over now. "Hey, we're going on the helter-skelter, come with us!"

They raced to the helter-skelter, grabbed some mats and scurried up the steps.

Up, and up, and up they went – higher than the tops of the trees! Then down they all whooshed, one after the other. . .

"WHEEE!"

Now, at long last, it was *toffee apple time*, so they hurried into the tent and all chose one.

"But mine's been nibbled! Look!" cried Starla.

"Ooooh," said Horatio, blushing. "I think I'd better have that one – swap you!"

Riley said they should eat them outside, as it was nearly time to be awarded the cup for winning the competition.

"Good idea," Starla smiled. "Let's go!"

She swapped her toffee apple for Horatio's un-nibbled one and they hurried back out. Podrick Hare was standing on a hay bale, and a crowd had gathered around him. Riley and his friends went over to join them.

"And now it's time," Podrick said, "to award the cup for best figurehead. And this year it goes to Horatio, Starla, Riley and Digby Mole!"

As they made their way to the front, the valley echoed with cheers. Then Podrick handed Riley a sparkly gold cup. They were allowed to keep it for the whole year, taking it in turns to have it in their cave-house.

"Thanks, Mr Hare," said Riley, smiling brightly.

They skipped off and showed the cup to Mimi-Rose, who liked sparkly things very much. Then Riley turned to Starla and Horatio and whispered something in their ears. All three of them nodded, then looked at Digby.

"Digby," said Riley, "me and the others want *you* to keep the cup all year long."

"*Me?*" Digby blinked and his cheeks turned bright pink.

"Yes," smiled Starla. "Ernest *was* your idea and we're sorry we didn't listen to you at first."

"Yeah, just because you've got a little voice," grinned Horatio, "that doesn't

mean you don't have big ideas!" They
passed him the shiny gold cup and
Digby beamed.

The friends sat on the riverbank eating their toffee apples, as fireflies danced above their heads.

"I *do* love Toffee Apple Night," said Riley. And this had been the best one ever!

Look out for more

stories — out now!

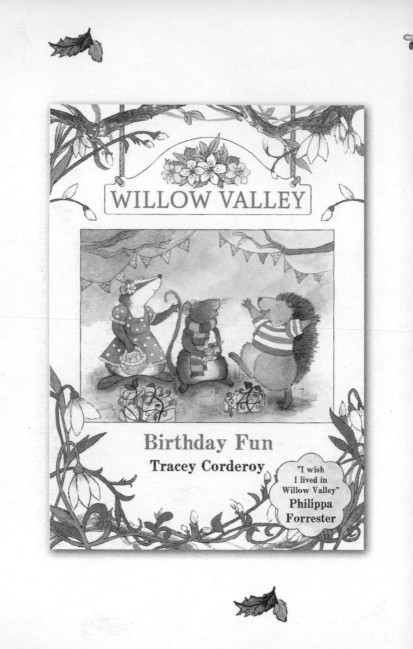

WILLOW VALLEY

Birthday Fun

Tracey Corderoy

"I wish
I lived in
Willow Valley"
**Philippa
Forrester**

WILLOW VALLEY

Spooky Sleepover

Tracey Corderoy

"I wish
I lived in
Willow Valley!"
**Philippa
Forrester**

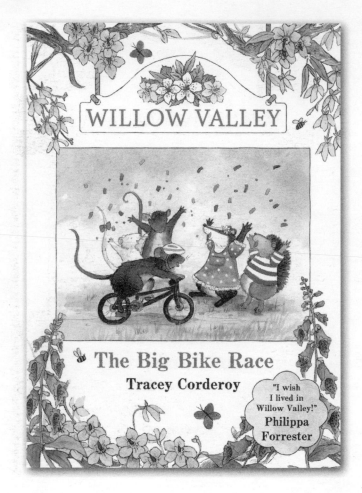

WILLOW VALLEY

The Big Bike Race
Tracey Corderoy

"I wish
I lived in
Willow Valley!"
**Philippa
Forrester**

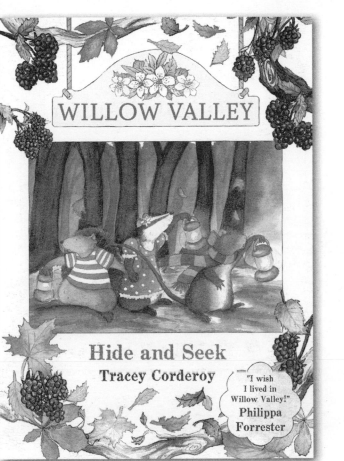

WILLOW VALLEY

Hide and Seek

Tracey Corderoy

"I wish
I lived in
Willow Valley!"
**Philippa
Forrester**

*Look out for the
special wintertime story*

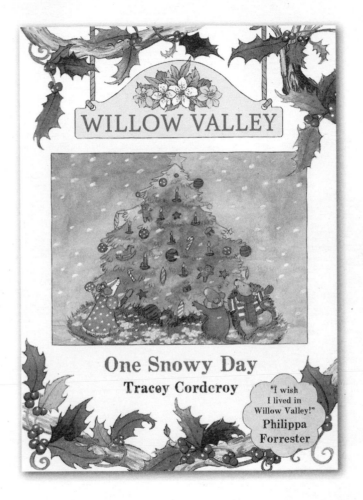

WILLOW VALLEY

One Snowy Day

Tracey Corderoy

"I wish
I lived in
Willow Valley!"
**Philippa
Forrester**

*Look out for the
special summertime story*

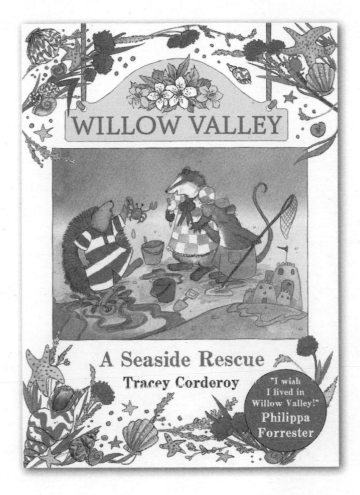

WILLOW VALLEY

A Seaside Rescue

Tracey Corderoy

"I wish
I lived in
Willow Valley!"
**Philippa
Forrester**